# Disney PLANES

# AIR POWER!

**Illustrated by the Disney Storybook Artists**

**A GOLDEN BOOK • NEW YORK**

ISBN 978-0-7364-3133-0
randomhouse.com/kids
MANUFACTURED IN CHINA
10 9 8 7 6 5 4 3 2 1

Dusty Crophopper is a crop duster from Propwash Junction.

Dusty dreams of being a racing plane.

Dusty's best friend is a fuel truck named Chug.

# Chug helps Dusty practice his racing.

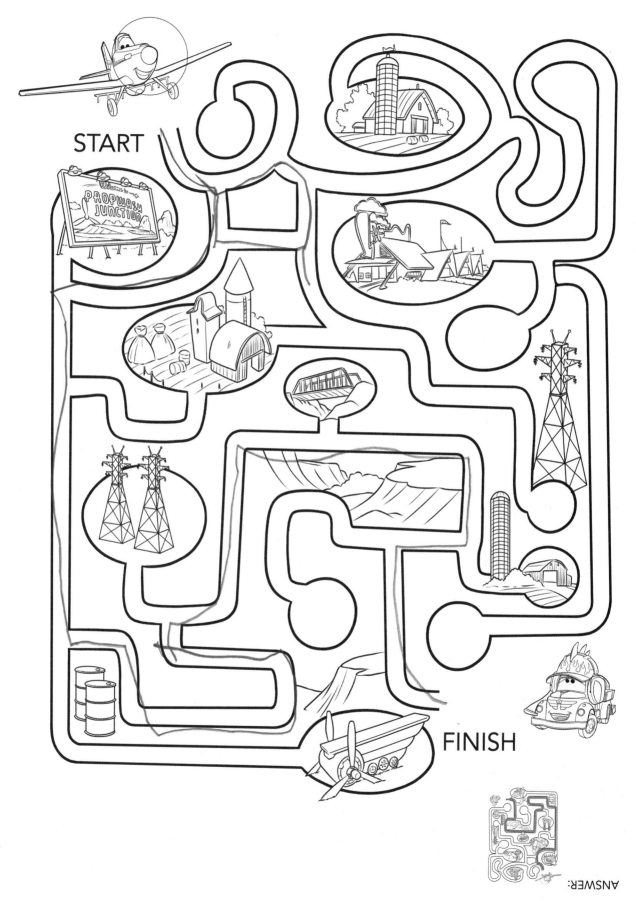

START

FINISH

ANSWER:

A plane named Skipper watches Dusty practice.

Dottie, a mechanic tug, keeps Dusty in top shape!

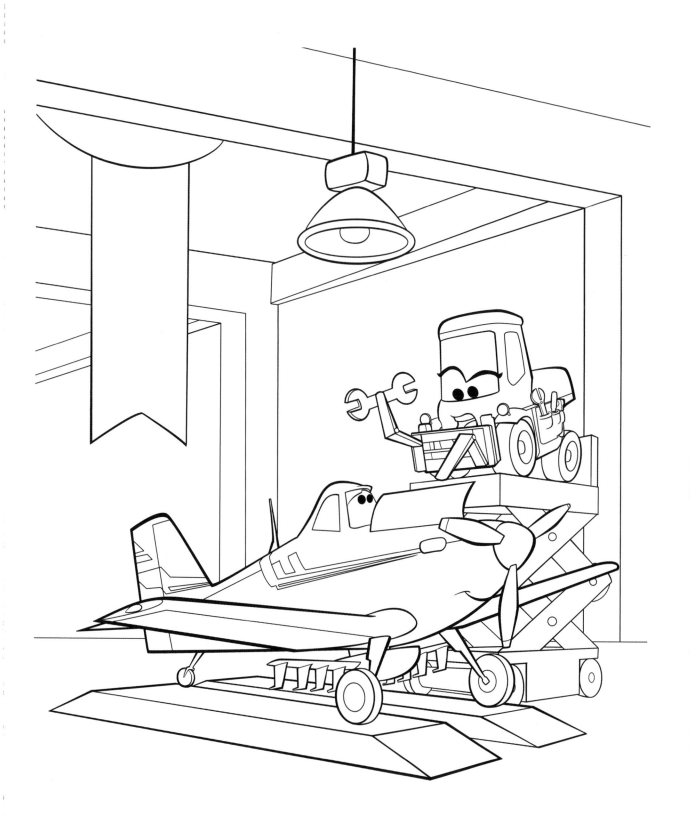

Dusty needs a trainer to help him get ready
for the Wings Around The Globe Rally.

Chug thinks Skipper could help Dusty train for the race.

Skipper was once a flight instructor, but he doesn't fly anymore.

Skipper tells Dusty to go away.

Ripslinger has won the Wings Around The Globe Rally three times!

To find out Ripslinger's nickname, start with the letter *T* and go around the circle twice, writing every other letter in order on the blanks.

__T__ __H__ __E__   __G__ __R__ __E__ __E__ __N__

__T__ __O__ __R__ __N__ __A__ __D__ __O__

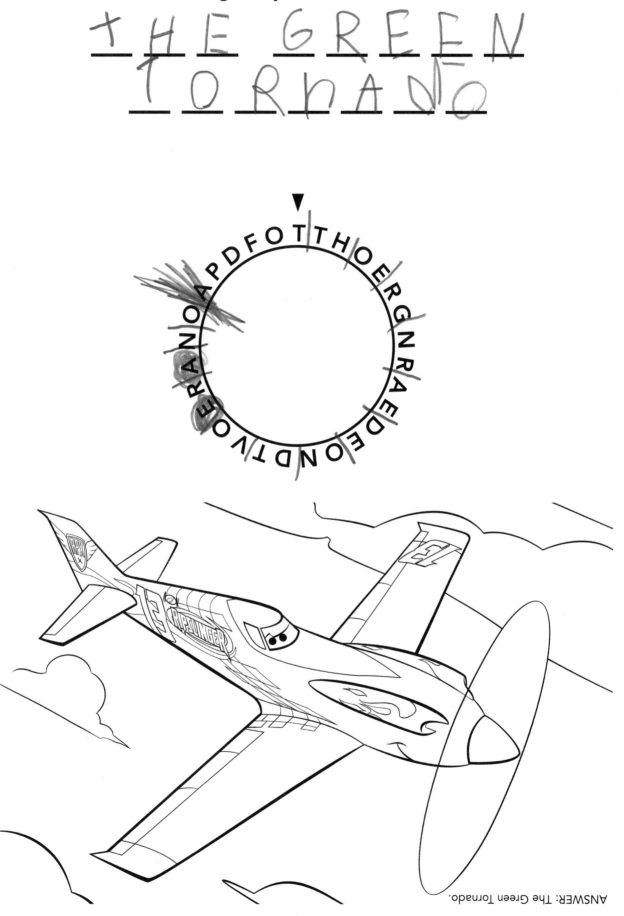

ANSWER: The Green Tornado.

The racers Ned and Zed are on Ripslinger's team.

Ripslinger doesn't have time for Dusty.

Ripslinger doesn't believe a crop duster like Dusty can fly in the race.

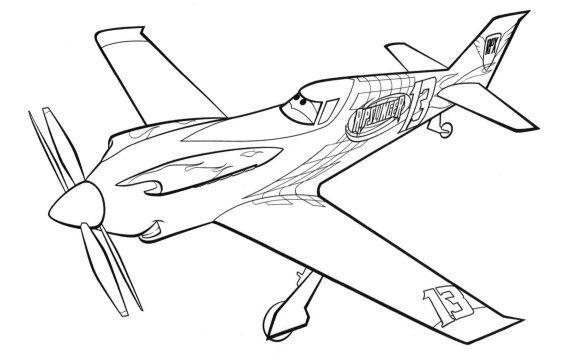

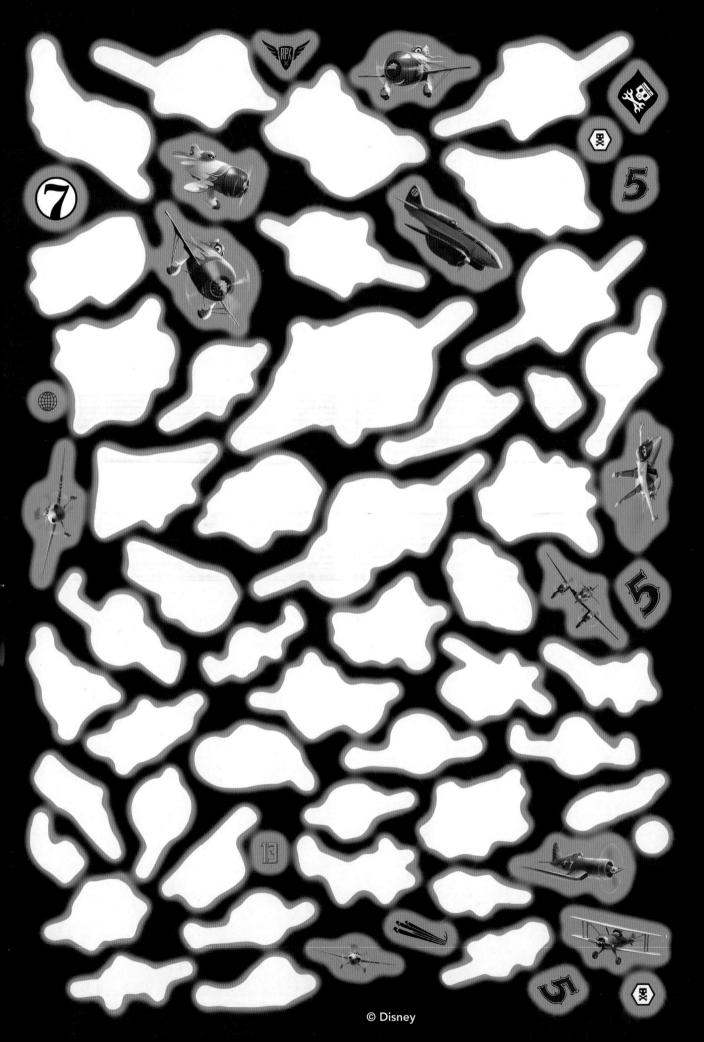

© Disney

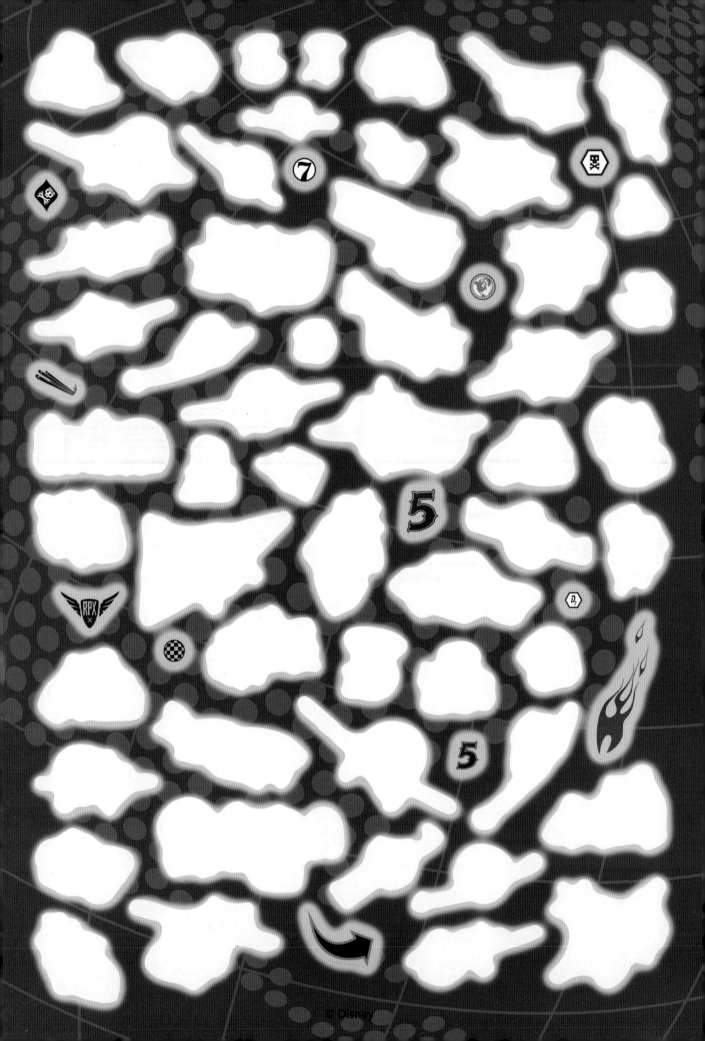

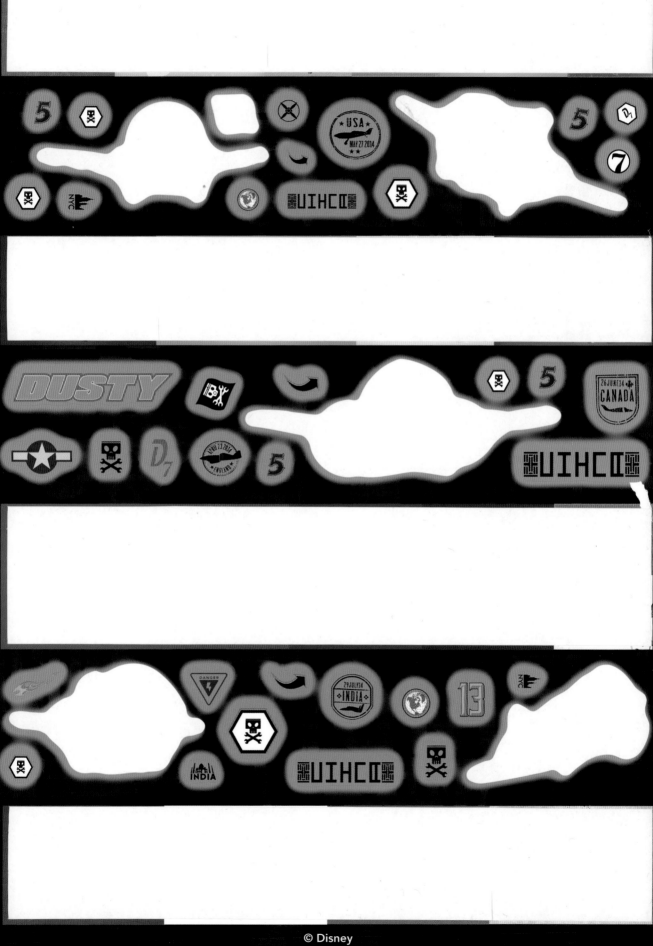

It's Dusty's turn to fly. He takes off and accidentally turns on his sprayer!

# Dusty flies faster than ever before!

# Help Dusty find the fastest path to the finish line.

FINISH

Dusty flies fast, but not fast enough to earn a spot in the race.

Dusty returns to Propwash Junction and tries to forget about racing.

When another racer drops out of the race,
Dusty is asked to take his place!

Skipper agrees to train Dusty, and they get ready for practice.

Skipper tells Dusty to fly up to the tailwinds,
but the crop duster is afraid of heights!

Solve the maze to help Dusty fly back to Skipper at the airfield.

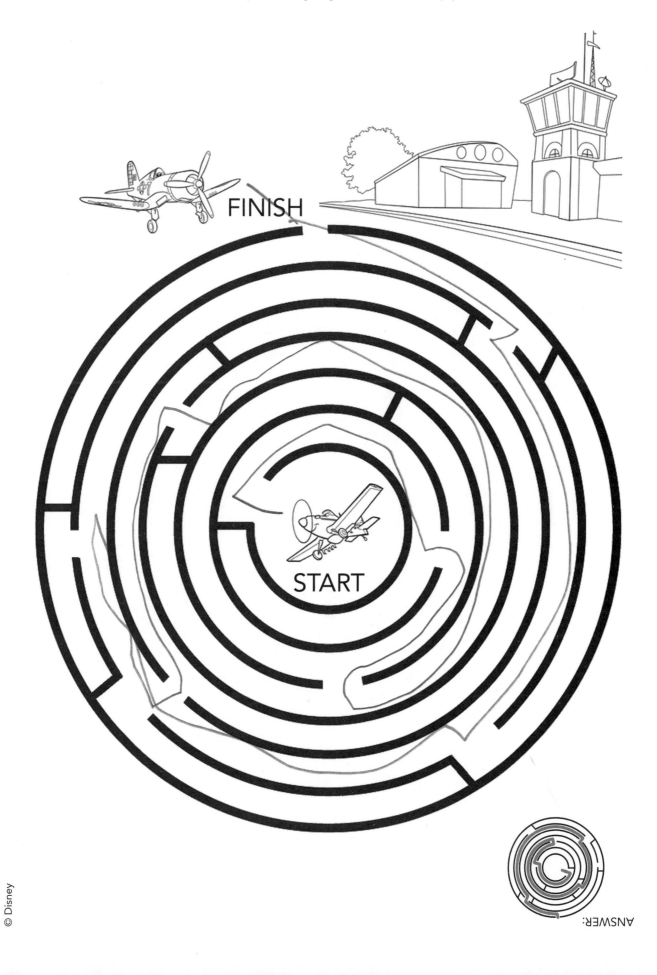

FINISH

START

ANSWER:

Skipper wants Dusty to overcome his fear of heights.

Dusty meets the other racers in the Wings Around The Globe Rally.

Bulldog is the racer from Great Britain.

Ishani comes from India.

The racer from Mexico wears a cape and a mask.

To learn his name, replace each letter with the one that comes before it in the alphabet.

e L    c h u v A C A B r A
F M    D I V Q B D B C S B

Dusty is the first crop duster to fly in the Wings Around The Globe Rally.

Rochelle is a rally champion from Canada.

© Disney

El Chu thinks Rochelle is beautiful.

# The Wings Around The Globe Rally begins!

Dusty flies low.

# Dusty is caught in a storm!
Help him fly through the iceberg maze and land safely in Iceland.

START

FINISH

Bulldog has oil in his eyes and can't see! But Dusty can help.
Find the line that leads Bulldog to Dusty.

Dusty and Bulldog land safely in Germany.

A German car named Franz has wings and can fly!

Dusty removes his heavy sprayer so he can fly faster.

Dusty flies low through the mountains of India.

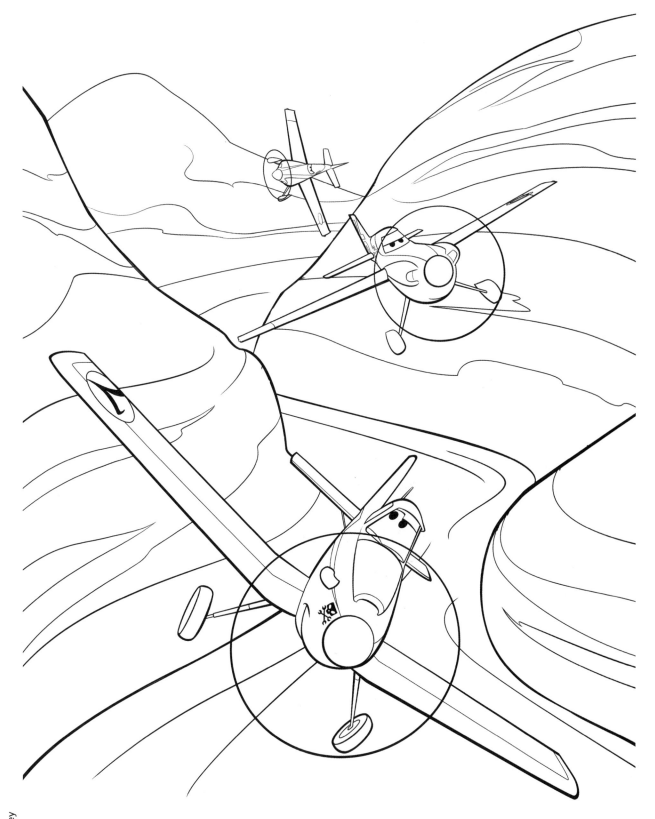

Ishani tells Dusty about a shortcut.

Dusty flies through a tunnel and almost runs into an oncoming train!

Dusty finds out that he has won the latest leg of the race!

Ripslinger wants to make sure that Dusty loses the next race.

Zed breaks off Dusty's antenna over the ocean!

Two fighter jets find Dusty just in time!

The captain gives the orders for Dusty to land.

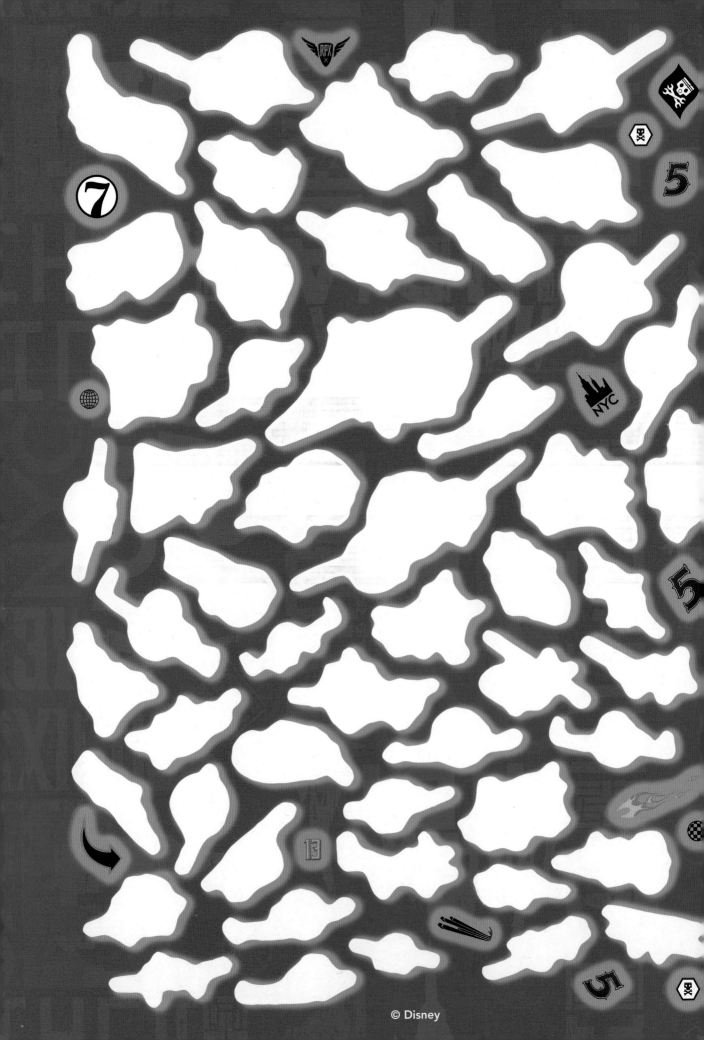

© Disney

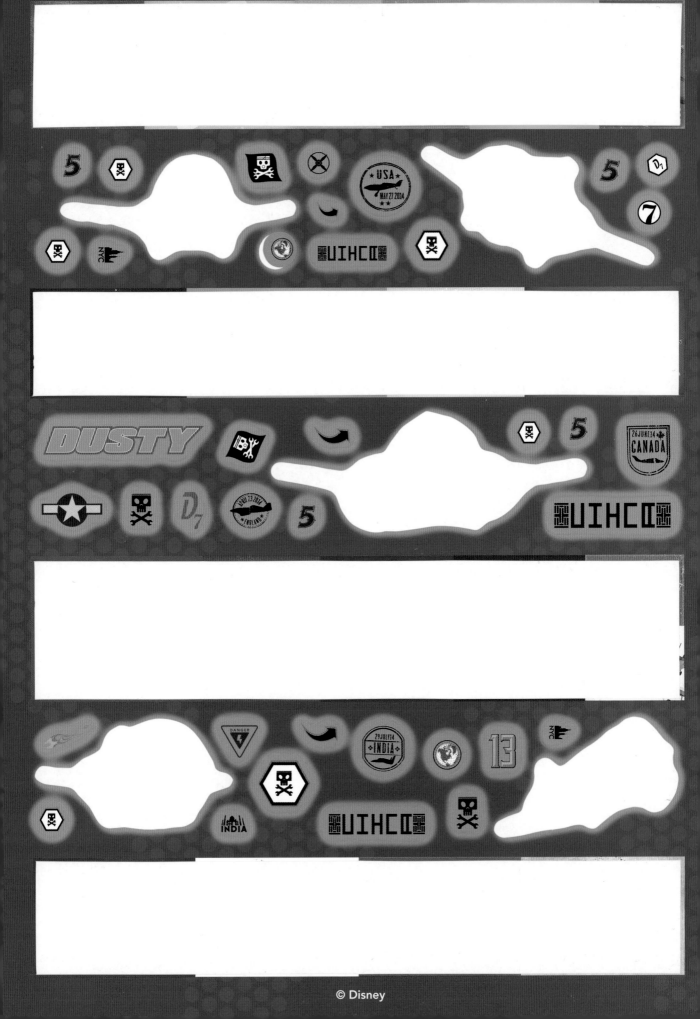

Dusty is repaired and refueled. He can get back in the race!

Whoo-hooo! Dusty flies toward Mexico.

During the storm, a giant wave crashes into Dusty!

Dusty arrives in Mexico, but his propeller is broken and his wings are cracked!

Dusty learns the truth about Skipper: he's afraid to fly!

Dusty's friends bring him new parts so
he can be repaired and fly again!

Dottie uses the new parts to turn Dusty into a real racer!

The final leg of the race begins. Ned and Zed try to make Dusty crash!

Skipper faces his fear—and flies to Dusty's rescue!

Ripslinger damages Skipper. The racer will do whatever it takes to win!

Dusty faces his own fear and flies into the tailwinds.
He flies higher and faster than ever before!

# Solve the maze to help Dusty catch up with Ripslinger.

START

FINISH

Ripslinger thinks he will win the race!

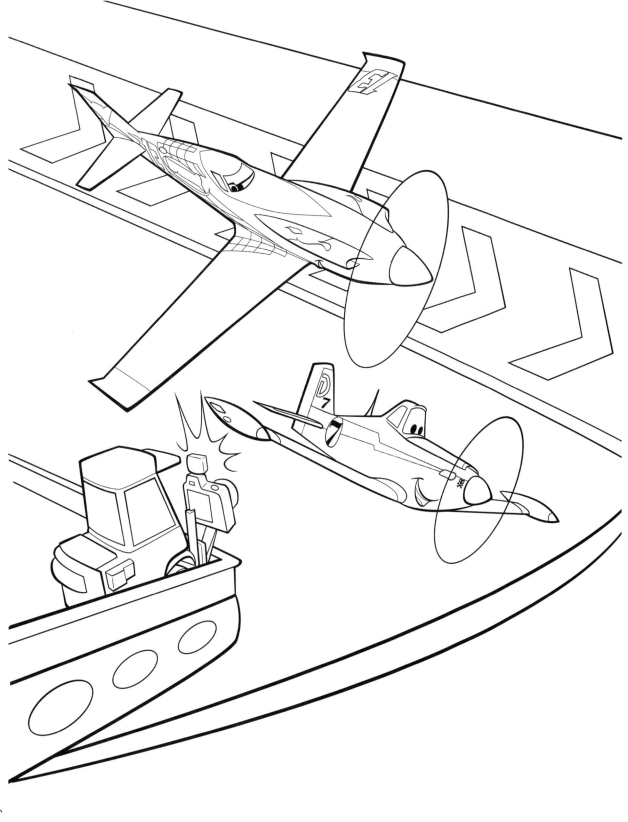

Dusty crosses the finish line first! He is the winner!

Dusty has become a racing champion!

Thanks to Skipper and his friends, Dusty's dream has come true!